D0284374

5 Minute Festive Stories

5 Minute Festive Stories

LITTLE TIGER PRESS

London

Contents

THE SMILEY SNOWMAN
M Christina Butler &
Tina Macnaughton

9

THE CHRISTMAS BEAR
Anne Mangan & Joanne Moss

37

THE LITTLE LOST ROBIN
Elizabeth Baguley & Tina Macnaughton

65

BLESS YOU, SANTA!
Julie Sykes & Tim Warnes

93

LITTLE BEAR'S SPECIAL WISH
Gillian Lobel & Gaby Hansen

121

RIDICULOUS!
Michael Coleman & Gwyneth Williamson

149

SANTA'S MAGIC KEY
Stephanie Stansbie & Emi Ordás

177

DEAR SNOWMAN
Kathryn White & Alison Edgson

205

The Smiley Snowman

M Christina Butler   Tina Macnaughton

The snowman was nearly finished. Little Bear and Small Fox lifted a big snowball on to his huge body.

"My turn!" cried Fluff Bunny. "Let me help!"

"Come on then, Fluff!" giggled Small Fox. "We can't leave you out!"

"Here we go!" cried Little Bear, lifting
him up, and Fluff gave the snowman
a great, big smile.

"Yippee!" squeaked Fluff. "He looks
really happy now! Hello, Snowman!"

"Let's go, Fluff!" shrieked Little Bear and
Small Fox, sliding down the hill.
    "But what about Snowman?" Fluff called.
"Don't worry, Snowman, I'll stay with
you. What shall we play?"

So together they played
snowballs . . .

and Fluff showed the
snowman how to do
headstands.

Then he told stories until
the sky grew dark and
snowflakes began to fall.

One by one, tiny lights started twinkling in the valley below.

"I have to go now," said Fluff. "Night-night, Snowman. See you tomorrow!"

15

Next morning the new snow sparkled bright.

"Wait for me!" gasped Fluff as he bounced up the hill after Little Bear and Small Fox.

But the snowman looked sad and shivery.

"Oh no!" whispered Fluff. "What's wrong?"

"He looks cold to me," said Little Bear. "He needs a hat!"

"I'll get a scarf!" cried Small Fox.

And off they went to see what they could find.

"This will warm him up!" giggled Little Bear as they pulled the woolly hat and scarf into place.

"What's happened to Fluff?" asked Small Fox
when they'd finished.

"I don't know," replied Little Bear. "But there's
something very strange coming up the hill! Look!"

"What can it be?" asked Small Fox,
hiding behind Little Bear.
A big, floppy thing with lumpy
bumps was shuffling nearer.
Suddenly Little Bear laughed.
"It's Fluff!" he yelled. "He's got a duvet!
Hold on, Fluff! We're coming!"

Together the friends pulled the duvet up to
the snowman. Then they tucked it round . . .
and pulled it up . . . and wrapped it round again . . .

until only the snowman's big pebble eyes were
peeping out.

"He'll be nice and cosy now," said Little Bear.
"Come on, Fluff. Small Fox has got a new sledge!"

Soon they were skimming
down the hill . . .

"We'll pull you, Fluff," laughed Little Bear. "Let's go and see Snowman."

with snowball fights on the way up — and down they went again — until Fluff was quite tired out and flopped back on the sledge!

25

But something was wrong!

Drip! Drip! Drip! Drops of water were running down the snowman's face, and there were puddles of water everywhere! "Our snowman's sinking!" Fluff yelled. "He's melting!" cried Little Bear. "We'll have to make him cold again!"

They pulled off the duvet, and threw his hat and scarf in the air.

"Don't worry, Snowman," cried Fluff. "We'll save you!"

"More snow! More snow!" shouted Little Bear as they padded and packed, and smoothed and patted.

Soon the snowman was bigger
and better than before.

"Wow!" gasped Little Bear. "We
nearly lost him!"

"But why does he still look
so *sad?*" puzzled Fluff, staring
up at the snowman.

Fluff stretched his arms as far as he could
around the snowman's big snow body.

"What's wrong, Snowman?" he asked
gently. "Please don't be so sad."

"Look," whispered Small Fox.
"Something is happening . . ."

"He's smiling!" cried Little Bear suddenly.

"Fluff's done it!" shouted Small Fox.

"Snowman wasn't cold on the outside.
He was cold on the inside!" Fluff grinned.
"He just needed a hug!"

And as the stars twinkled in the clear
night sky, they gave the snowman another
hug and his happy smile grew bigger
than ever!

The Christmas Bear

Anne Mangan

Joanne Moss

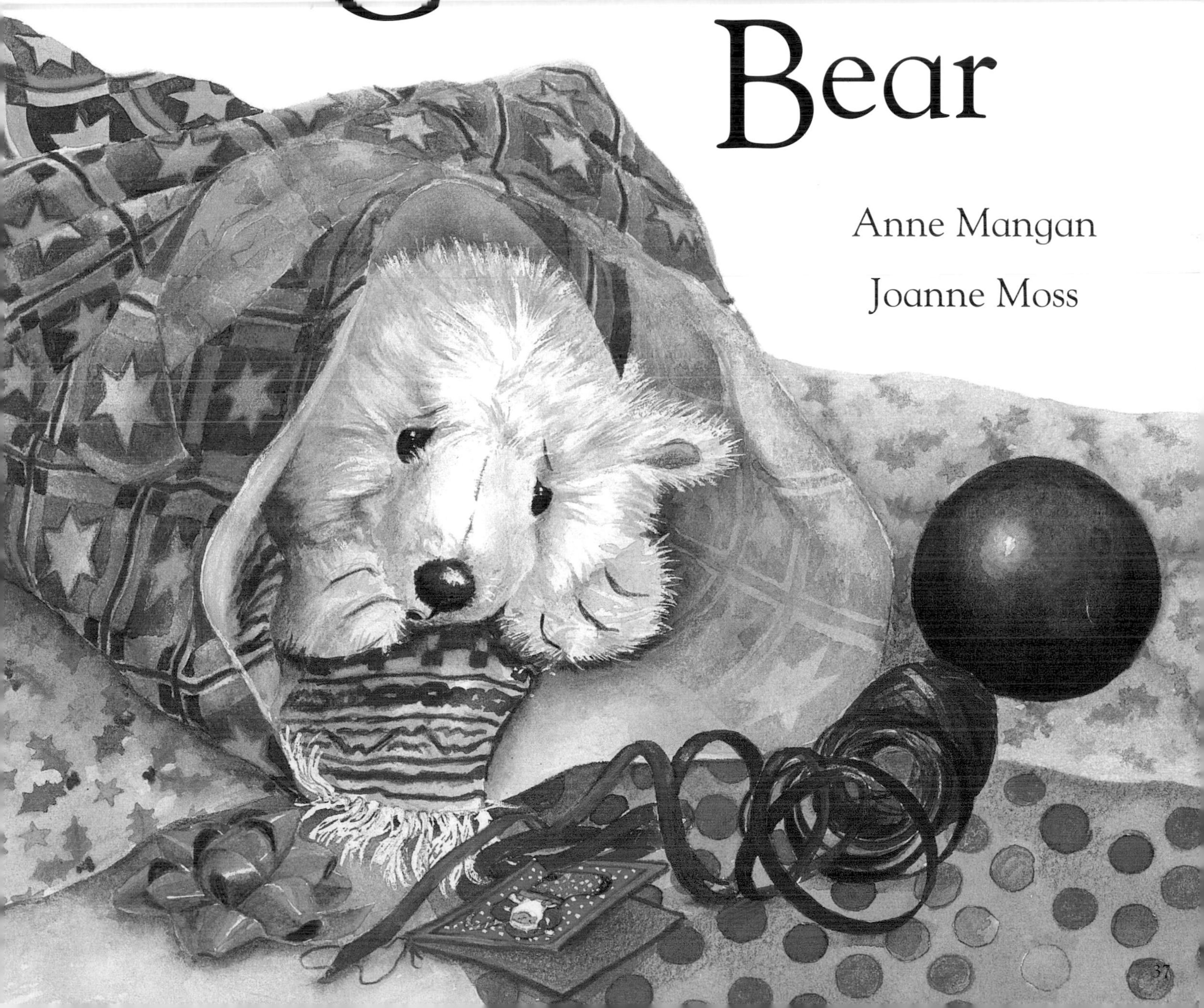

It was nearly Christmas and it was snowing.
Inside the toy shop there was a little polar bear.

Now that it was Christmas he hoped that he
would get a home at last. He had been waiting
for a long time.

But the assistant picked him up. "That bear won't sell," she said. And she placed him up on a high shelf, between a yellow monkey and a big doll.

"If you're in the shop for too long
they put you up here," whispered
the monkey.

"But it's okay," said the big doll.
"We can see a lot of things
from up here."

But the little bear just
wished for a home.

44

"I have an idea," said
the monkey suddenly.
He wriggled off the shelf,
right into a child's arms!

"You could do that," the doll
told the little polar bear.
"I'd be too afraid," he said.
"I daren't either," said the
doll. "I would break."
So they sat side by side
and waited and hoped . . .

A week before Christmas a lady and a little
boy came into the shop.

"I need a present for my sister Becky,"
the little boy said.

"How about this bear?"
asked the assistant.

"He looks like a mistake," said the lady rudely. "People will think we got him cheap." They chose a calculator instead.

The little bear felt very sad.
He flopped right over, but
someone picked him up,
gave him a shake, and
set him back in
his place.

The next day a girl came into the shop. She saw the doll on the high shelf. "Exactly what I've been looking for," she cried.
The big doll was overjoyed.

The little polar bear missed the big doll dreadfully. He sat on his high shelf all alone, while people came in and out of the shop in a last minute rush to buy their presents for Christmas.

He saw so many toys being sold, and he wanted a home more than ever. If only someone would choose him!

It seemed as though the little polar bear's wish was granted, for suddenly someone looked up at him and said, "What a jolly little bear. I'll give him to my daughter."

The little polar bear was delighted. He couldn't wait to see his new home.

But the little girl wasn't happy.
"I don't want a silly bear," she cried.
"I wanted a racing car!"
She threw the little bear
across the room.

So the little bear was taken
back to the shop, and put
back up on the high shelf
once more.

He felt worse than ever.

He had given up all
hope of ever being
wanted and loved.

On Christmas Eve a man and a woman with cheerful faces came into the shop.

"We're looking for a Christmas present for our niece, Elly," said the woman.

"How about this little bear?" said the man, taking
down the polar bear. "He's nice and soft."
"Yes, I think Elly will like him." the woman replied.

The little polar bear felt happy and afraid, all at the same time. "Suppose Elly doesn't like me?" he thought. He worried and worried as he was wrapped up in a Christmas parcel for the next day.

On Christmas morning, Elly's aunt and uncle gave her an extra special present.

Elly felt the parcel. It was very soft, like something she wanted to hug.

Then she opened it. Elly looked at the little bear and the little bear looked at Elly.

"He's the nicest present I've ever had!" Elly cried,
and she buried her face in his soft fur.
Elly took the little polar bear outside to let
him see the snow. Now he had a home and
someone to give him lots and lots of hugs.
He was the happiest little bear
in the world!

The Little
Lost Robin

Elizabeth Baguley   Tina Macnaughton

On the edge of the deep wood lived an old hare. Once, he had leapt and pranced under the magical moon, but time had made him grey and stiff, and he no longer danced. Instead he spent his time looking out over the world, gently daydreaming.

68

Every day, Hare went to feed the small
brown birds, who chattered and chirruped.
Remembering his long-ago moondancing,
Hare tapped a merry paw to their busy tunes.
    One morning, in swooped a bird with
a berry-bright breast. "You're a bold
little robin," laughed Hare.

Even when autumn came, Hare still went
to share food with his friends. But then
a chill wind scattered the leaves, and the
birds, too cold to stay, flew far away.
Their song echoed with goodbye.
"I'll miss you, little birds," sighed Hare.

Then something made Hare prick up his ears.
A song! A song that lilted faintly, away in
the wood. It was a bird! Hare hurried towards
the fir tree where Robin shone scarlet, singing
a song warm as summer.

"Robin! You didn't fly away!" exclaimed Hare.

And as Robin sang brightly, Hare wound round in a slow dance.

"You've made this old hare feel young again," he laughed.

So, every day, Hare would walk into the blustery woods to bring Robin seeds and sway to her song.

When winter arrived, freezing the wood and stiffening Hare's legs, Robin would come to the burrow to see him. Hare would wake as soon as the sun rose, and wait for her so that they could eat breakfast together.

"What would I do without you?" smiled Hare.

Then came a night that howled with storm-fury. A wild wind exploded into the wood, blasting and splintering trees. In whirled the snow, hiding the land under its biting cold whiteness.

Deep in his burrow, Hare could not sleep for worry about Robin. Had she been blown into the storm, homeless and afraid?

At first light Hare rushed outside, hoping that Robin would be waiting for him. But there was no Robin, no Robin anywhere! Where was she? Why hadn't she come? Hare had to try to find her.

81

Out into the
snowy wood Hare
struggled. Finally he came
to Robin's tree and stopped.
It lay fallen, wrenched from the
ground by the storm.
"Robin!" he gasped. "Where are you?"
But, searching through the branches,
Hare found only her empty nest.

He slumped down, sure
that Robin was lost.

Just then, a tiny cheep made him look up.

"Robin!" Hare shouted in amazement. "I thought the storm had taken you!"

As fast as she could, Robin flew to him.

"It's all right, little one," Hare said gently.
"You can come back with me. I'll plant your
tree outside my burrow, so you'll be quite
at home."

The sun sank slowly as
Hare trudged home. Over
the humps and hollows of
snow he went, with Robin
nestled safely on his shoulder.

Back home, Hare helped Robin make a new
nest in the fir tree's branches. Every day
she warbled and whistled, and when the
night brought the light of the magical
moon, Hare joyfully danced to her
winter-bright tunes.

Bless You, Santa!

Julie Sykes   Tim Warnes

It was very nearly Christmas and
Santa was up early.

"Jingle bells, jingle bells," he sang
cheerfully. "Breakfast first and then to work."

He filled the kettle and put on toast, but
as he poured cereal into his bowl Santa's nose
began to tickle.

"*Aah, aah, AAH . . .*"

DECEMBER
23

94

"Atishoo!"

he roared. His sneeze blew
ccreal all over the place.

"Bless you, Santa," said Santa's cat, shaking cornflakes out of her tail. "That's a nasty cold."

"Dear me, no!" said Santa in alarm. "It can't be! It's nearly Christmas. I haven't got time for a cold!"

After breakfast Santa rushed to his workshop
and set to work on the unfinished toys. Merrily
he sang as he painted a robot. But Santa's sneezes
were growing larger and louder.

"Aah, aah, AAH . . ."

"Atishoo!"

"Bless you, Santa," squeaked Santa's little mouse, gathering the beads his sneezes had scattered.

"Bless you, Santa," said Santa's cat, chasing paper stars as they fluttered around. "You sound awful. Go and sit by the fire."

"I feel awful!" snuffled Santa. "But I can't rest yet. It's nearly Christmas and I have to finish these toys or there will be no presents for all the . . . *Aah, aah, AAH . . .*"

"Atishoo!"

Santa sneezed so hard that he slipped over and landed in a stack of balls. Down the balls tumbled, bouncing off Santa and bopping around the room. They crashed into cars, they pushed over paint pots, they toppled the teddies and *ruined* the rockets.

"Atishoo!"

"Just look at this terrible mess!" wailed Santa. "I'll never be ready in time for Christmas now!"

"Go to bed, Santa," ordered Santa's little mouse. "You're not well. Your nose is so red the reindeer could use it to guide your sleigh! We'll clear up this mess and get everything ready for Christmas."

So Santa's mouse put Santa
back to bed with a mug of hot milk
and a little something to help the cold.
Santa huddled under his duvet.
He sneezed . . . "Atishoo!"

He snuffled . . .

And finally he snored.

sssh!

zzzzzzZZZZZZZZZZ Z Zzzzzzzzzzzz

Meanwhile, back in the workshop,
Santa's friends worked as hard as they
could. They mopped . . .

They mended . . .

They glued . . .

They snipped, they stuck and they wrapped. Faster and faster they toiled until every single present was finished. Then sleepily they stumbled off to bed.

Next evening, as the sun set, the animals waited with a sleigh piled high with toys.

"But where is Santa?" asked Santa's cat. "I hope he's better!"

"Who's going to drive the sleigh and deliver all the presents?" asked the reindeer.

"Listen," said Santa's cat. "Can you hear something?"

The animals listened.

"It's Santa!" squealed Santa's little mouse. "Are you better, Santa? Can you deliver the presents?"

Santa wrinkled his nose.

"Aah, aah, AAH . . ."

"Ha ha haaa!" chuckled Santa loudly.

"Only joking! I feel much better. Bless you, everyone. You did a great job! Thanks to you all I will get these presents delivered in time for Christmas day."

Santa climbed aboard his sleigh. "Reindeer, up, up and AWAY!" he shouted.

It was a busy night as Santa flew
around the world delivering presents.

When at last Santa landed back at the North Pole
the sun was rising. But he hadn't finished yet.

"These presents are for you," said Santa.

"Presents for us!" squeaked Santa's cat.

"Th . . . Th . . . THAA . . ."

"Atishoo!"

Santa's cat sneezed so hard that a pile of
snow fell off the trees and buried everyone.
"Bless you!" laughed Santa. "And a
Happy Christmas to you too!"

119

Little Bear's Special Wish

Gillian Lobel

Gaby Hansen

The sun was still in bed when
Little Brown Bear crept out into
the shadowy woods.

"I wish, I wish . . ." he whispered.

"You're up early, Little Brown Bear!" called
Lippity Rabbit. "What are you wishing for?"

"It's my mummy's birthday," said Little
Brown Bear, "and I wish I could find the most
special present in all the world for her."

"I'll help you!" said Lippity Rabbit.
So off they went along the winding path. Little
pools of moonlight danced around their feet.

In the middle of the woods was a big rock.

Little Brown Bear sat down for a moment to
think. High above him glittered a star, so big and
bright he could almost touch it.

"I know – I could give my mummy a star,"
he said. "That would be a very special present."

Little Brown Bear gave
a little jump. But he could
not reach the star.

He gave a very big jump.
But still he could not reach
the star. Then Little Brown
Bear had an idea.

"I know!" he said. "If we climb to the very top of the hill, then we will be able to reach the stars!"

From the top of the hill the stars looked even brighter – and much nearer, too. Little Brown Bear stretched up on to his tiptoes. But the stars were still too far away. Then Little Brown Bear had a very good idea indeed.

"I know!" he said. "We must build
a big, big tower to the stars!"
   "I'll help you!" said
Lippity Rabbit.

Together they piled the biggest stones they could find,
one on top of the other. Then they stepped back and
looked. A stone stairway stretched to the stars.
   "Now I shall reach a star for my mummy," said Little
Brown Bear happily. He climbed right to the top and
stretched out a paw. But still he couldn't reach the stars.

"I know!" called Lippity Rabbit. "If I climb on your shoulders, then I can knock a star down with my long, loppy ears!"

Lippity Rabbit scrambled on to Little Brown Bear's shoulders. He stretched up his long, loppy ears. He waggled them furiously.

"Be careful, Lippity!" called Little Brown Bear. "You're making me wobble!"

Suddenly Little Brown Bear felt
something tapping his foot.

"Can I help you?" croaked a voice.

"Why yes, Very Small Frog," said
Little Brown Bear. "Are you any good
at jumping?"

Very Small Frog puffed out his chest.
"Just watch me!" he said. High into
the air he flew, and landed right
between Lippity Rabbit's long,
loppy ears.

"Can you reach the
brightest star from there?"
asked Little Brown Bear.

"No problem!" shouted Very Small Frog.
He took a mighty breath. "Look out,
stars, here I come!" he shouted.

Very Small Frog gave a great push with his strong
back legs. Up, up, up he sailed. Lippity Rabbit's
long, loppy ears twirled round and round.

"Help!" he shouted. "Somebody save me!"

Backwards and forwards he swayed, and backwards
and forwards swayed Little Brown Bear. With a
mighty crash the stone tower toppled to the ground.
And down and down tumbled Lippity Rabbit and
Little Brown Bear.

"I can't breathe, Lippity!" gasped Little Brown Bear. "You're sitting right on by dose!"

Then Very Small Frog sailed down from the stars and landed on Lippity Rabbit's head.

"I'm sorry, Little Brown Bear," he said. "I jumped right over the moon, but I still couldn't reach the stars."

Little Brown Bear sat up carefully. His nose was scratched and his head hurt.

"Now my special wish will *never* come true," he said. "I shall never find a star for my mummy!"

"Don't be sad, Little Brown Bear," said Lippity Rabbit. And he gave him a big hug.

A tear ran down Little Brown Bear's nose, and splashed into a tiny pool at his feet.

As he rubbed his eyes, Little Brown Bear saw something that danced and sparkled in the shining water. Surely it was his star! Little Brown Bear jumped up with excitement.

"Now I know what to do!" he cried.

Off he ran down the hillside.
"Wait for us!" cried Lippity Rabbit
and Very Small Frog.

Through the ferny woods they ran, over the silver meadows, until they reached the stream. For a long time they hunted along the sandy shore until Little Brown Bear found just what he was looking for. Then carefully, carefully, he carried it all the way home.

"Happy birthday, Mummy!" he cried.

Into his mother's lap he placed a pearly shell that shone like a rainbow. There, in the heart of the shell, a tiny pool of water quivered. And in that pool a very special star shimmered and shook – the star that had made a little bear's birthday wish come true.

"Lippity Rabbit and Very Small Frog helped me find the shell, but I caught the star all by myself!" said Little Brown Bear proudly.

Mother Bear knelt down and gave him a big hug.

"Thank you all very much," she said. "This is a very special birthday present indeed!"

Ridiculous!

Michael Coleman   Gwyneth Williamson

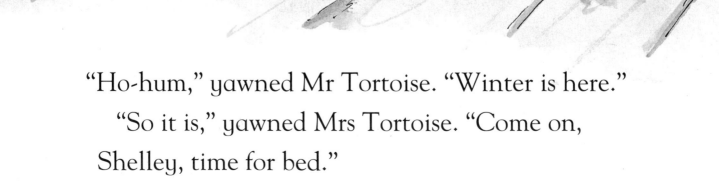

"Ho-hum," yawned Mr Tortoise. "Winter is here."
"So it is," yawned Mrs Tortoise. "Come on,
Shelley, time for bed."

"But I don't feel sleepy yet," said Shelley.

"*Ridiculous!*" cried Mr Tortoise. "All tortoises
go to sleep for the winter."

"Why?" asked Shelley.

"Because it's cold outside and there's no food."

"But I don't want to go to sleep," said Shelley. "I want to see what winter is like!"

"*Ridiculous!*" cried Mr and Mrs Tortoise together. "Whoever heard of a tortoise outside in winter?"

Soon
Mr Tortoise
began to snore . . .

and not long after
that Mrs Tortoise
began to snore . . .

and not long after *that*, Shelley left her warm bed of leaves, and out she went through a hole in the shed to see what winter was like.

Outside the shed, Shelley blinked.

There was snow and ice everywhere, even on the duck pond and the hill. As she lumbered along a duck spotted her.

"A tortoise out in winter?" quacked the duck. "*Ridiculous!*"

"No it isn't," said Shelley.

"Oh no? Then let me see you break through the ice to get food like *I* can. Ha-quack-ha!"

"He's right," thought Shelley. "I can't do that. I don't have a beak."

As Shelley began to walk up the hill, she met a dog.

"A tortoise out in winter?" barked the dog. "*Ridiculous!*"

"No it isn't," said Shelley, feeling a bit cross.

"Oh no? Then let's see you keep warm by running around like *I* can. Ha-woof-ha!"

"He's right," thought Shelley sadly. "I can't do that either."

The dog ran off after a cat, but the cat
jumped on to the branch of a tree.
She looked down at Shelley.

"A tortoise out in winter?" miaowed the cat. "*Ridiculous!*"

"No it isn't," said Shelley, even more crossly.

"Oh no? Then let me see you run into a nice warm house as quickly as *I* can. Ha-miaow-ha!"

"She's right," thought Shelley, shivering with cold. "I can't run like a dog or a cat. I'm much too slow!"

The cat raced off into her house before the dog could catch her, and Shelley trudged on up to the top of the hill, where she met a bird.

"A tortoise out in winter?" cheeped the bird. "*Ridiculous!*"

"No it isn't," snapped Shelley.

"Oh no? Then let me see you fly off home to cuddle up with your family like *I* can. Ha-cheep-ha!"

"Of course I can't fly," thought Shelley. "I can't even hop!"

Shelley felt cold and miserable. She remembered her lovely warm bed and a tear trickled down her cheek.

"They're *all* right," she thought. "A tortoise out in winter *is* ridiculous!"

Sadly she crept behind a shed where nobody could see her crying . . .

and slipped on a big patch of ice! Shelley fell over
backwards and began to slide down the hill.
Faster and faster she went . . .

. . . faster than

a *dog* could run . . .

faster than

a *cat* . . .

until suddenly she
hit a bump . . .

and flew into the air
like a *bird*.

Wheeee!

Down she came again and landed on the icy duck
pond. She slithered towards her hole in the shed . . .

but it was all covered up with ice!

"Ha-quack-ha, what did I say? Where's your beak to break the ice with?" The duck fell about laughing.

"I don't have a beak," thought Shelley. "But I *do* have . . .

"*. . . a shell!*"
And tucking her head inside it,
Shelley smashed her way through the ice,
into the shed and home!

Mrs Tortoise woke up as she heard all the noise.

"You haven't been outside, have you, Shelley?" she asked.

"Outside?" said Shelley, snuggling into bed. "Whoever heard of a tortoise out in winter?"

And before you could say
"Ridiculous!"
Shelley was fast asleep.

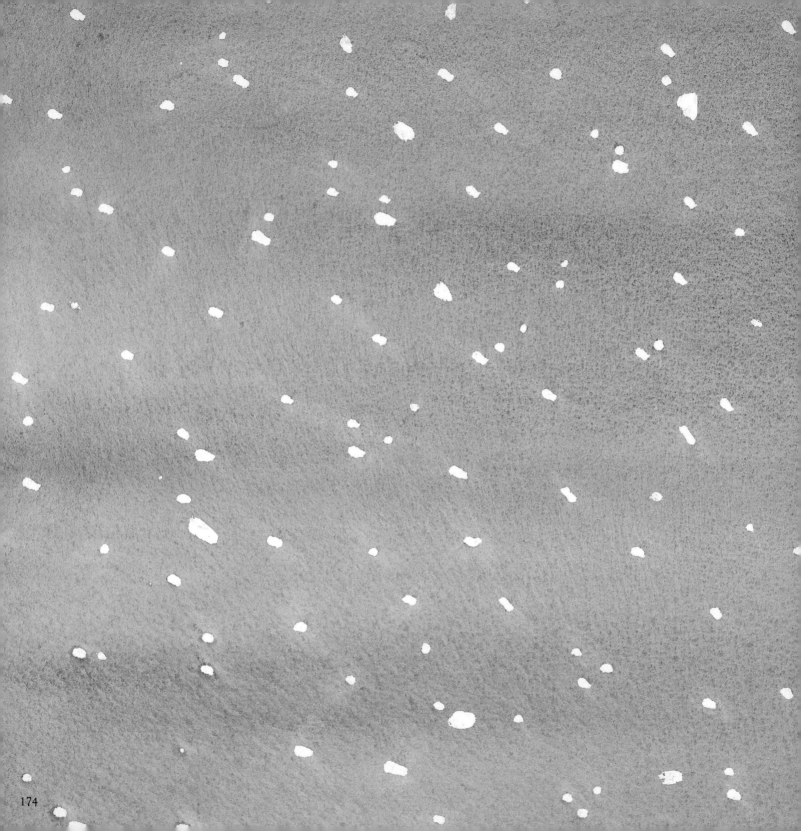

Santa's Magic Key

Stephanie Stansbie   Emi Ordás

It was Christmas Eve
and Pip the dog was 'helping'
Milo decorate. He raced round and
round, tying himself up in tinsel and barking
at the baubles.

"Silly Pip!" said Milo. "Tinsel goes on the tree!
It's got to look extra good for our brand new house."

"Wow!" said Milo's dad, coming in
with a plate of biscuits. "You and Pip
did a great job!"

"Oooh, yum!" Milo squealed.

"Hands off! These are for
Santa," laughed Mum.

"But Santa can't have too many," Milo explained, "or his tummy will get big and then he'll get stuck in the . . ."

Suddenly Milo had a terrible thought. "We don't have a chimney. Santa won't be able to get in! How will he bring our presents?"

"What are we going to do, Pip?" cried Milo. "We've got to find Santa!"

"Where are you off to?" asked Dad.

"The North Pole, of course!" said Milo.

Dad scratched his head. "That's a very long walk, Milo. And it's nearly time for bed."

"But if Santa can't come down the chimney,"
cried Milo, his bottom lip wobbling, "we won't get
any presents!"

"Don't you worry about that," said Mum, giving
Milo a big cuddle. "Santa always finds a way –
you'll see. But he can't come unless you're in bed.
Come on!" And she marched him up the stairs.

Soon Milo was tucked up under the covers. But he couldn't sleep – he just kept thinking about Santa.

"Oh, Pip, this is the worst Christmas ever!"

Then he noticed Pip snuffling about under the bed.
"What have you found?" asked Milo.

Pip barked and pushed out a small wooden box.
Carved into the top was a magnificent flying
reindeer.

Slowly Milo lifted up the lid. Inside
was a huge golden key.

"Wow!" he whispered. "Hang on
a minute – there's a label . . ."

"Mum! Dad!" Milo hollered, racing down the stairs. "Look what Pip found. It's a key from Santa!"

"Wow!" said Mum. "Let's go and hang it outside."

"It looks too big for our lock," worried Milo.

"Don't worry," said his mum. "It's a magic key that only works for Santa."

"Will he definitely see it?" asked Milo. "Maybe I should sleep downstairs – just in case."

"Nice try," chuckled Dad, and he bundled him back up to bed.

"Let's stay awake and wait for Santa!" whispered
Milo to Pip. "I want to make sure he finds the
magic key."

Pip barked and jumped up by the window
to keep watch. Milo sat up in bed and
started waiting.

But it wasn't long before he drifted off to sleep . . .

Pip watched the stars twinkling in the dark.
Suddenly his ears pricked up as a jingle
of bells rang out through the night.
Then . . .

W h o o s h !

Santa's sleigh swept across the sky.
It whizzed up into the air and dived down again
to land softly on the snow outside.

Pip ran downstairs to the front door. There was
a tinkling sound in the lock, then slowly,
the door creaked
open . . .

Pip looked up at a perfectly round, red tummy, past
a huge white beard, and into Santa's smiling face. It
was really him! Pip barked with delight.

"Ho, ho, ho!" chuckled Santa and patted Pip on
the head. "I'll need your help with all these presents.
There's quite a lot here, you know!"

Early on Christmas morning, Milo raced downstairs yelling, "Pip! Pip! Did Santa find the key?"

Pip was dozing, surrounded by presents, with the magic key nestled in his paws.

"Yessss!" squealed Milo. And he gave Pip a great big cuddle.

"Hurray for Santa!" Mum cheered, as she and Dad shuffled in, yawning.

"Your mum was right," smiled Dad. "Santa always finds a way."

Soon the air was filled with laughter and flying wrapping paper. And Christmas in their new home was the most magical ever.

Dear
Snowman

Kathryn White   Alison Edgson

Little Rabbit had made
a wonderful, smiley snowman.
   "Hello, Snowman," said Little Rabbit,
wrapping him in a snuggly scarf. "Do you
want to play?"

All winter long, Little Rabbit
played with Snowman.
He showed him how to
feed the birds . . .

and how to throw snowballs!

Every evening, when the first stars twinkled,
he hugged Snowman tight and whispered,
"Night-night, Snowman. See you tomorrow."

209

Then one morning, when
Little Rabbit ran out to play,
Snowman was gone!

"Snowman!" called Little Rabbit.
"Where are you?" But all he
could hear was the plop of melting
snow, tumbling from the trees.

Little Rabbit raced indoors. "Mummy, Mummy! Snowman has gone!" he cried.

"Don't worry," smiled Mummy, scooping him up. "I'll tell you a big secret. In spring, all snowmen go on holiday. Snowman will be back next winter."

"Really?" gasped Little Rabbit. "My snowman's gone on holiday!"

A few weeks later, Little Rabbit was watering his carrot patch when Postman arrived.

"A postcard for Little Rabbit," he called.

"For me?" Little Rabbit exclaimed.

He laughed with delight as he read the postcard with Mummy.

Dear Little Rabbit,
It's very hot here in the desert. Did you know that some camels have one hump, and some have two? Riding them is very bumpy and lots of fun!
Wish you were here.

Love,
Snowman xx

FAR FAR AWAY · FAR FAR AWAY

Little Rabbit
Corner Cottage
Berry Lane

"My snowman's been riding a camel!" Little Rabbit giggled.

That night, Little Rabbit
dreamed that Snowman lifted him
high up onto a camel. They galloped
across the shimmering sand together.
It was the best dream ever!

Little Rabbit was playing with Mole one sunny morning, when Mummy called him. "Little Rabbit, come quick! Snowman has sent you another postcard."

"Yippee!" cried Little Rabbit, racing over.

Dear Little Rabbit,
I am having great
adventures in the jungle.
A naughty monkey took
my hat! Did you know that
monkeys eat flowers as
well as bananas?
Missing you,
Snowman xxx

Little Rabbit
Corner Cottage
Berry Lane

"I wonder if Snowman got his hat back?" said Mole.

"Of course!" exclaimed Little Rabbit. "My snowman is fast . . .

and brave . . .

and very clever!

And he'd get his hat
back EASILY!"

More and more postcards
arrived for Little Rabbit.
He looked at the bright
pictures and wondered
what adventure Snowman
would have next.

Then one autumn morning another postcard arrived with a picture of a rushing waterfall. "It's beautiful here," Mummy read, "but I miss you, Little Rabbit. I'm coming home soon."

"Snowman is coming home!" cried Little Rabbit, dancing through the golden leaves. "Will he be here today?"

"Not today," said Mummy, "but in winter, when the soft snow falls. Just you wait and see."

"Oh, when will it snow?" wondered Little Rabbit, watching the fluffy clouds float across the sky.

Then one evening,
as Little Rabbit peeped
out of his bedroom window,
he saw soft white flakes
drifting down.

"Hurry home, Snowman!"
he whispered.

That night, as Little Rabbit
slept, the snow fell faster
and faster. And something
wonderful happened . . .

Snowman came home!

5 MINUTE FESTIVE STORIES

LITTLE TIGER PRESS
1 The Coda Centre,
189 Munster Road,
London SW6 6AW
www.littletiger.co.uk

First published in Great Britain 2016

This volume copyright © Little Tiger Press 2016
Cover artwork copyright © Emi Ordás 2016
All rights reserved

Printed in China • LTP/1800/1523/0516

ISBN 978-1-84869-333-3

2 4 6 8 10 9 7 5 3 1

THE SMILEY SNOWMAN

M Christina Butler
Illustrated by Tina Macnaughton

First published in Great Britain 2010
by Little Tiger Press

Text copyright © M Christina Butler 2010
Illustrations copyright © Tina Macnaughton 2010

THE CHRISTMAS BEAR

Anne Mangan
Illustrated by Joanne Moss

First published in Great Britain 1999
by Little Tiger Press

Text copyright © Anne Mangan 1999
Illustrations copyright © Joanne Moss 1999

THE LITTLE LOST ROBIN

Elizabeth Baguley
Illustrated by Tina Macnaughton

First published in Great Britain 2007
by Little Tiger Press

Text copyright © Elizabeth Baguley 2007
Illustrations copyright © Tina Macnaughton 2007

BLESS YOU, SANTA!

Julie Sykes
Illustrated by Tim Warnes

First published in Great Britain 2004
by Little Tiger Press

Text copyright © Julie Sykes 2004
Illustrations copyright © Tim Warnes 2004
Visit Tim Warnes at www.ChapmanandWarnes.com

LITTLE BEAR'S SPECIAL WISH

Gillian Lobel
Illustrated by Gaby Hansen

First published in Great Britain 2003
by Little Tiger Press

Text copyright © Gillian Lobel 2003
Illustrations copyright © Gaby Hansen 2003

RIDICULOUS!

Michael Coleman
Illustrated by Gwyneth Williamson

First published in Great Britain 1996
by Little Tiger Press

Text copyright © Michael Coleman 1996
Illustrations copyright © Gwyneth Williamson 1996

SANTA'S MAGIC KEY

Stephanie Stansbie
Illustrated by Emi Ordás

First published in Great Britain 2015
by Little Tiger Press

Text copyright © Little Tiger Press 2015
Illustrations copyright © Emi Ordás 2015

DEAR SNOWMAN

Kathryn White
Illustrated by Alison Edgson

First published in Great Britain 2013
by Little Tiger Press

Text copyright © Kathryn White 2013
Illustrations copyright © Alison Edgson 2013